Mattie's Magical Garden

Jan Davis

AuthorHouse™
1663 Liberty Drive
Bloomington, IN 47403
www.authorhouse.com
Phone: 1 (800) 839-8640

Because of the dynamic nature of the Internet, any web addresses or links contained in this book may have changed since publication and may no longer be valid. The views expressed in this work are solely those of the author and do not necessarily reflect the views of the publisher, and the publisher hereby disclaims any responsibility for them.

Any people depicted in stock imagery provided by Getty Images are models, and such images are being used for illustrative purposes only.
Certain stock imagery © Getty Images.

This book is printed on acid-free paper.

ISBN: 978-1-7283-2511-8 (sc)
ISBN: 978-1-7283-2512-5 (hc)
ISBN: 978-1-7283-2510-1 (e)

Library of Congress Control Number: 2019912731

Print information available on the last page.

Published by AuthorHouse 08/30/2019

authorHOUSE®

Mattie's Magical Garden

Mattie's garden was a wonderful place, filled with color and life. All who passed by would stop and stare at the beautiful flowers.

Mattie was a very happy soul and took joy in the beauty of her garden.

There were daisies, and mums, tulips and daffodils, one long tall row of sunflowers and many assorted pansies, but the most beautiful of all the flowers were the roses.

The roses were in a group of their own, red and yellow, pink and white, all fighting for Mattie's attention, all trying to be the best of the bunch.

Over in the corner, away from the rest, was one lonely little rose bush struggling for the water and sunlight. The water from the sprinklers did not quite reach this tiny rose bush, and it was over shadowed by the other larger bushes that were in full bloom with all their varied colors.

Mattie had a little girl that would play every afternoon in the garden after school. The little girl loved the garden and felt like a fairy princess. She pretended all the flowers were her faithful subjects and Mattie would let her pick one flower each Friday to keep her company through the weekend.

The summer months passed quickly, the little rose bush pushed it's roots down deep in order to reach the water at the edge of the garden.

Most of the flowers had bloomed by now and were fading as time passed, while the little rose bush had gone unnoticed by both Mattie and the little girl.

This did not deter the little rose bush however, as it continued to grow deeper and stronger, stretching for the sunlight between the other rose bushes.

Each Friday the fairy princess would pick another flower as her favorite subject for the weekend, it would set in the blue vase by her bed and be the first thing she saw in the morning and the last thing she saw at night.

Many days went by and there was no activity in the garden. Mattie was busy with other things and the flowers had all but faded with the onset of the winter months ahead.

The little girl was not available either, as she had developed a fever and could no longer play outside. How she missed those summer days and her faithful flower subjects, but she was just too weak and laid in her bed staring at the cold empty room.

Mattie wished there was a way to make her little girl smile again. She remembered those happy days in the garden and the vision of the fairy princess with her faithful flower subjects.

One evening, while walking through the garden, Mattie noticed that all the flowers that were so rich in color only months before seemed to be asleep, waiting for the winter cold to tuck them in. All that is except the little rose bush at the corner of the garden. Never before had Mattie seen such color as if it had been kissed by the sun, small and perfect it had the greenest leaves and the softness peddles, just like velvet.

For this little rose bush had worked twice as hard and taken twice as long to bloom as the other flowers, but now stood alone as the most beautiful flower in the garden.

The next morning when the little girl awoke, instead of the cold empty room she had seen the night before, the room was filled with sunlight and hope. The last of her faithful flower subjects had reached the blue vase at the side of her bed and greeted her with a smile that would warm her heart and renew her spirit.

Childhood memories stay with us forever, as well as the love of family. This story is based on the author's great grandmother's actual garden, and lessons learned about natural beauty and survival. It has been written in memory of a magical time gone by and never forgotten.